"The Mysterious Story of Al Kahf (Ar Raqim)"

Abdul Waheed

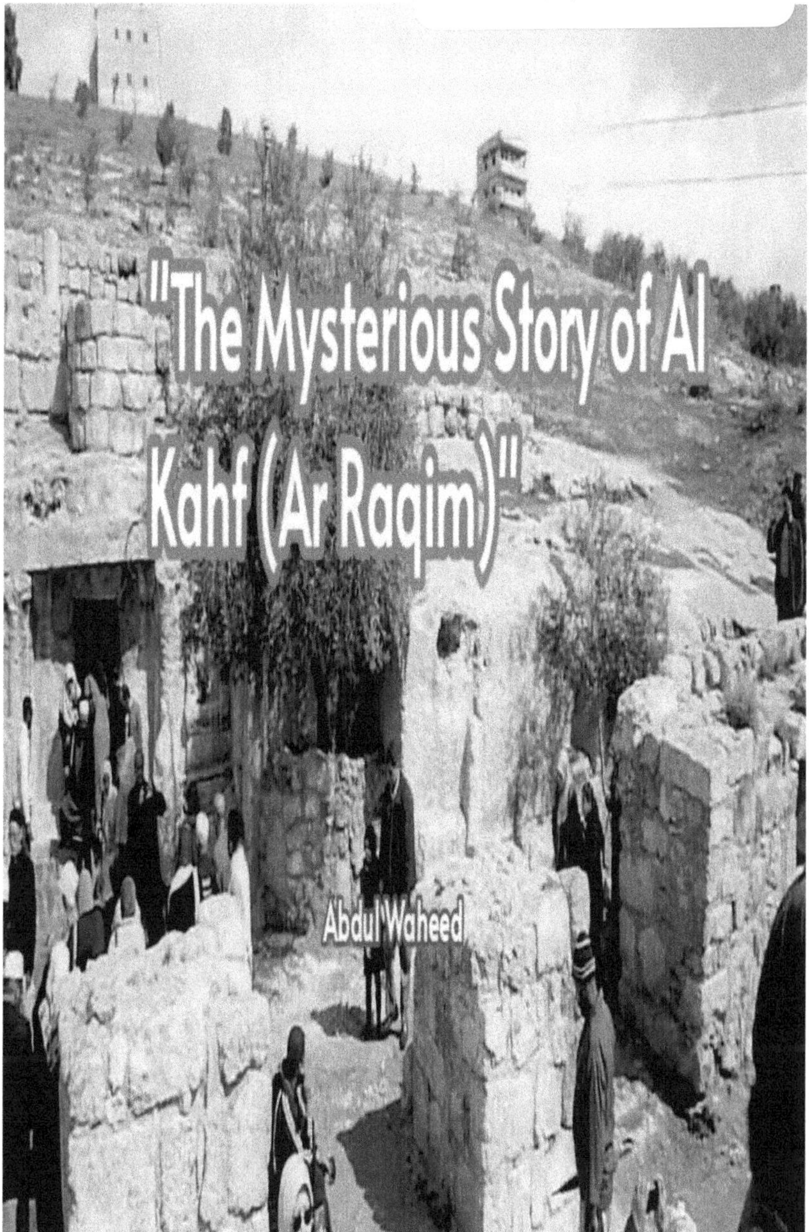

"The Mysterious Story of Al Kahf (Ar Raqim)"

Abdul Waheed

© **Abdul Waheed**

No copying of this book with out permission

Dedication

This book is dedicated to the memory of my late father Haji Ubairdur Rahman (Munna) and younger brother Abdul Hameed. May God (Allah) give peace to his soul.

Aamen

Table of contents

Preface

In this book there is a discussion of a mysterious cave called Alkahaf Ar Raqim. Whose mention is in the Holy Quran and it is historical, because the government and other scientists have discovered this which has been found to be true, this incident is strange because this incident is mentioned in the Holy Quran that they were some young men who Had gone to the cave and slept for 309 years, a very surprising incident. Read this and let me know if you want to add any other topic, Thanks,

Yours - Abdul Waheed, Barabanki, UP, India.

Date- 09/01/2023

surah al kahf
أَصحابَ الكَهفِ كون تهى
AL QURAN KAREEM
كهف أهل الكهف
(بورجوفية) وردت تضم فى القـرآن الكـريم
CAVE OF THE SEVEN SLEEPERS
BYZANTINE TOMBS _ ONE MENTIONED
IN THE KORAN IN THE STORY OF THE
SEVEN SLEEPERS
Hosted by Sentiasapanas.com

In holy Quran

(سورة الكهف)

٩) أَمْ حَسِبْتَ أَنَّ أَصْحَابَ الْكَهْفِ وَالرَّقِيمِ كَانُوا مِنْ آيَاتِنَا عَجَبًا

١٠) إِذْ أَوَى الْفِتْيَةُ إِلَى الْكَهْفِ فَقَالُوا رَبَّنَا آتِنَا مِنْ لَدُنْكَ رَحْمَةً وَهَيِّئْ لَنَا مِنْ أَمْرِنَا رَشَدًا

١١) فَضَرَبْنَا عَلَىٰ آذَانِهِمْ فِي الْكَهْفِ سِنِينَ عَدَدًا

١٢) ثُمَّ بَعَثْنَاهُمْ لِنَعْلَمَ أَيُّ الْحِزْبَيْنِ أَحْصَىٰ لِمَا لَبِثُوا أَمَدًا

١٣) نَحْنُ نَقُصُّ عَلَيْكَ نَبَأَهُمْ بِالْحَقِّ إِنَّهُمْ فِتْيَةٌ آمَنُوا بِرَبِّهِمْ وَزِدْنَاهُمْ هُدًى

١٤) وَرَبَطْنَا عَلَىٰ قُلُوبِهِمْ إِذْ قَامُوا فَقَالُوا رَبُّنَا رَبُّ السَّمَاوَاتِ وَالْأَرْضِ لَنْ نَدْعُوَ مِنْ دُونِهِ إِلَٰهًا لَقَدْ قُلْنَا إِذًا شَطَطًا

١٥) هَٰؤُلَاءِ قَوْمُنَا اتَّخَذُوا مِنْ دُونِهِ آلِهَةً لَوْلَا يَأْتُونَ عَلَيْهِمْ بِسُلْطَانٍ بَيِّنٍ فَمَنْ أَظْلَمُ مِمَّنِ افْتَرَىٰ عَلَى اللَّهِ كَذِبًا

١٦) وَإِذِ اعْتَزَلْتُمُوهُمْ وَمَا يَعْبُدُونَ إِلَّا اللَّهَ فَأْوُوا إِلَى الْكَهْفِ يَنْشُرْ لَكُمْ رَبُّكُمْ مِنْ رَحْمَتِهِ وَيُهَيِّئْ لَكُمْ مِنْ أَمْرِكُمْ مِرْفَقًا

١٧) وَتَرَى الشَّمْسَ إِذَا طَلَعَتْ تَزَاوَرُ عَنْ كَهْفِهِمْ ذَاتَ الْيَمِينِ وَإِذَا غَرَبَتْ تَقْرِضُهُمْ ذَاتَ الشِّمَالِ وَهُمْ فِي فَجْوَةٍ مِنْهُ ذَٰلِكَ مِنْ آيَاتِ اللَّهِ مَنْ يَهْدِ اللَّهُ فَهُوَ الْمُهْتَدِ وَمَنْ يُضْلِلْ فَلَنْ تَجِدَ لَهُ وَلِيًّا مُرْشِدًا

١٨) وَتَحْسَبُهُمْ أَيْقَاظًا وَهُمْ رُقُودٌ وَنُقَلِّبُهُمْ ذَاتَ الْيَمِينِ وَذَاتَ الشِّمَالِ وَكَلْبُهُمْ بَاسِطٌ ذِرَاعَيْهِ بِالْوَصِيدِ لَوِ اطَّلَعْتَ عَلَيْهِمْ لَوَلَّيْتَ مِنْهُمْ فِرَارًا وَلَمُلِئْتَ مِنْهُمْ رُعْبًا

١٩) وَكَذَٰلِكَ بَعَثْنَاهُمْ لِيَتَسَاءَلُوا بَيْنَهُمْ قَالَ قَائِلٌ مِنْهُمْ كَمْ لَبِثْتُمْ قَالُوا لَبِثْنَا يَوْمًا أَوْ بَعْضَ يَوْمٍ قَالُوا رَبُّكُمْ أَعْلَمُ بِمَا لَبِثْتُمْ فَابْعَثُوا أَحَدَكُمْ بِوَرِقِكُمْ هَٰذِهِ إِلَى الْمَدِينَةِ فَلْيَنْظُرْ أَيُّهَا أَزْكَىٰ طَعَامًا فَلْيَأْتِكُمْ بِرِزْقٍ مِنْهُ وَلْيَتَلَطَّفْ وَلَا يُشْعِرَنَّ بِكُمْ أَحَدًا

٢٠) إِنَّهُمْ إِنْ يَظْهَرُوا عَلَيْكُمْ يَرْجُمُوكُمْ أَوْ يُعِيدُوكُمْ فِي مِلَّتِهِمْ وَلَنْ تُفْلِحُوا إِذًا أَبَدًا

وَكَذَٰلِكَ أَعْثَرْنَا عَلَيْهِمْ لِيَعْلَمُوا أَنَّ وَعْدَ اللَّهِ حَقٌّ وَأَنَّ السَّاعَةَ لَا رَيْبَ فِيهَا إِذْ يَتَنَازَعُونَ (٢١)
بَيْنَهُمْ أَمْرَهُمْ ۖ فَقَالُوا ابْنُوا عَلَيْهِم بُنْيَانًا ۖ رَبُّهُمْ أَعْلَمُ بِهِمْ ۚ قَالَ الَّذِينَ غَلَبُوا عَلَىٰ أَمْرِهِمْ لَنَتَّخِذَنَّ
عَلَيْهِم مَّسْجِدًا

سَيَقُولُونَ ثَلَاثَةٌ رَّابِعُهُمْ كَلْبُهُمْ وَيَقُولُونَ خَمْسَةٌ سَادِسُهُمْ كَلْبُهُمْ رَجْمًا بِالْغَيْبِ ۖ (٢٢)
وَيَقُولُونَ سَبْعَةٌ وَثَامِنُهُمْ كَلْبُهُمْ ۚ قُل رَّبِّي أَعْلَمُ بِعِدَّتِهِم مَّا يَعْلَمُهُمْ إِلَّا قَلِيلٌ ۗ فَلَا تُمَارِ فِيهِمْ إِلَّا
مِرَاءً ظَاهِرًا وَلَا تَسْتَفْتِ فِيهِم مِّنْهُمْ أَحَدًا

وَلَا تَقُولَنَّ لِشَيْءٍ إِنِّي فَاعِلٌ ذَٰلِكَ غَدًا (٢٣)

إِلَّا أَن يَشَاءَ اللَّهُ ۚ وَاذْكُر رَّبَّكَ إِذَا نَسِيتَ وَقُلْ عَسَىٰ أَن يَهْدِيَنِ رَبِّي لِأَقْرَبَ مِنْ هَٰذَا (٢٤)
رَشَدًا

وَلَبِثُوا فِي كَهْفِهِمْ ثَلَاثَ مِائَةٍ سِنِينَ وَازْدَادُوا تِسْعًا (٢٥)

قُلِ اللَّهُ أَعْلَمُ بِمَا لَبِثُوا ۖ لَهُ غَيْبُ السَّمَاوَاتِ وَالْأَرْضِ ۖ أَبْصِرْ بِهِ وَأَسْمِعْ ۚ مَا لَهُم مِّن (٢٦)
دُونِهِ مِن وَلِيٍّ وَلَا يُشْرِكُ فِي حُكْمِهِ أَحَدًا

[Quran Chapter 18]

9. Did you know that the People of the Cave and the Inscription were of Our wondrous signs?

10. When the youths took shelter in the cave, they said, "Our Lord, give us mercy from Yourself, and bless our affair with guidance."

11. Then We sealed their ears in the cave for a number of years.

12. Then We awakened them to know which of the two groups could better calculate the length of their stay.

13. We relate to you their story in truth. They were youths who believed in their Lord, and We increased them in guidance.

14. And We strengthened their hearts, when they stood up and said, "Our Lord is the Lord of the heavens and the earth; we will not call

on any god besides Him, for then we would have spoken an outrage."

15. "These people, our people, have taken to themselves gods other than Him. Why do they not bring a clear proof concerning them? Who, then, does greater wrong than he who invents lies and attributes them to Allah?"

16. "Now that you have withdrawn from them, and from what they worship besides Allah, take shelter in the cave. And your Lord will unfold His mercy for you, and will set your affair towards ease."

17. You would have seen the sun, when it rose, veering away from their cave towards the right, and when it sets, moving away from them to the left, as they lay in the midst of the cave. That was one of Allah's wonders. He whom Allah guides is truly guided; but he whom He misguides, for him you will find no directing friend.

18. You would think them awake, although they were asleep. And We turned them over to the right, and to the left, with their dog stretching its paws across the threshold. Had you looked at them, you would have turned away from them in flight, and been filled with fear of them.

19. Even so, We awakened them, so that they may ask one another. A speaker among them said, "How long have you stayed?" They said, "We have stayed a day, or part of a day." They said, "Your Lord knows best how long you have stayed." "Send one of you to the city, with this money of yours, and let him see which food is most suitable,

and let him bring you some provision thereof. And let him be gentle, and let no one become aware of you."

20. "If they discover you, they will stone you, or force you back into their religion; then you will never be saved."

21. So it was, that We caused them to be discovered, that they would know that the promise of Allah is true, and that of the Hour there is no doubt. As they were disputing their case among themselves, they said, "Build over them a building." Their Lord knows best about them. Those who prevailed over their case said, "We will set up over them a place of worship."

22. They will say, "Three, and their fourth being their dog." And they will say, "Five, and their sixth being their dog," guessing at the unknown. And they will say, "Seven, and their eighth being their dog." Say, "My Lord knows best their number." None knows them except a few. So do not argue concerning them except with an obvious argument, and do not consult any of them about them.

23. And never say about anything, "I will do that tomorrow."

24. Without saying, "If Allah wills." And remember your Lord if you forget, and say, "Perhaps my Lord will guide me to nearer than this in integrity."

25. And they stayed in their cave for three hundred years, adding nine.

26. Say, "Allah knows best how long they stayed." His is the mystery of the heavens and the earth. By Him you see and hear. They have

no guardian apart from Him, and He shares His Sovereignty with no one.

According to Tafsir

The easiest interpretations of the words of the Most High / Abu Bakr Al-Jazairi (b. 1921 AD)

Interpretation of Aasr al-Tafsir of the words of the Most High/Abu Bakr al-Jaza'iri (d. 1921 AD),

Abu Bakr al-Jazaeri

Abu Bakr Jabir bin Musa bin Abdul Qadir ibn Jaber, better known as Abu Bakr al-Jazairi (1921 – 15 August 2018), was an Algerian Sunni Islamic scholar.

Biography– Al-Jazairi was born in 1921 in the village of Lioua, close to Tolga, which is located today in the state of Biskra Province in Algeria. In his hometown grew up and received his primary education, and began to memorize the Quran and some Almtun language and jurisprudence of Maliki, and then moved to the city of Biskra, where started to teach in a private school. Then he traveled with his family to Medina, and in the Prophet's Mosque resumed his education way to sit to the circles of scholars and sheikhs where he got permission from the Presidency of the judiciary in Mecca to teach in the Prophet's Mosque. He worked as a teacher in some schools of the Ministry of Education and in Dar Al Hadith in Madinah. When the Islamic University of Madinah opened its doors in 1961, he was one of its first teachers and teachers, and remained there until he retired in 1987.

He was under the teachings of sheiks as Naim Al-Nuaimi, Issa Mutawqi and Tayeb Al-Aqbi in Algeria, and Omar Berry and Mohammed Al-Hafiz in Medina. One of his disciples was Saleh Al Maghamsi.

Abu Bakr al-Jazairi was widely known for teaching in the Prophet's Mosque for 50 years and in Islamic University of Medina, which earned his lessons and books great momentum. His book The Platform of the Muslim is one of his most widely accepted works in the Arab countries. He refused to compliment by the financial sector and warned against riba in his book to the prayers. He wrote a book in particular his advice to every Shiite.

He died in Medina on Wednesday 15 August 2018 at the age of 97.

Before leaving Algeria he was involved in politics and participated in the Bayan party. He also participated in the establishment of the

Unionist Youth Movement, a unitary Islamic movement, later known for his opposition to the Houari Boumédiène regime. After settling in Saudi Arabia, he focused on the scientific side without forgetting to talk about ideological and politics. He declared his opposition to atoning the Muslim rulers and exiting them. He believed that all this was achieved only in the light of the Quran and Sunnah. In the jihad, he was against the Soviet occupation of Afghanistan in the 1980s.

Barren desert: that is, dirt without plants, so barren land is dirt and barren soil that has no plants.

Al-Kahf: The wide grove in the mountain and the narrow one in it is called "Ghar".

Al-Raqim: a stone tablet on which the names of the Companions of the Cave are inscribed.

The young men took refuge in the cave: they took it as a shelter for themselves and a house in which they stayed.

Al-Fatayya: The plural of young men is young believers.

Provide us with guidance in our affairs: that is, facilitate for us the path of guidance and guidance.

So we struck their ears: that is, we struck a veil over their ears that prevents them from hearing sounds and movements.

Number of years: that is, several years.

Then We raised them: that is, from their sleep, meaning We woke them up.

Calculate how long they stayed: that is, determine the times of their resurrection in the cave.

Term: any limited, known period.

Meaning of the verses:

God Almighty says: {Indeed, We have made all that is on the earth an adornment for it} of animals, trees, plants, rivers and seas, and His saying: {We will surely test them} meaning that We may test them {which of them is best in deed} meaning which of them I should leave it and follow our commands and prohibitions and work in it in obedience to us, and His saying: {And Indeed, We will make what is upon it a barren level ground.} That is to say, we will destroy it one day, after it has been built up, fresh, and decorated. We will make it {a barren desert land}, that is, dust with no vegetation. Therefore, do not be sad, O our Messenger, and do not be distressed by what you encounter from your people, for the fate of life is because of it. They have attacked you and disobeyed us, until you become barren land. And God Almighty says: {Or did you consider that the Companions of the Cave and Ar-Raqim were a wonder of Our signs? Jaba} that is, it was more impressive than Our signs in He created and created things, the heavens and the earth, and even among God's creations, there are things that are much more amazing. And his saying: {When the young men took refuge in the cave} This is the beginning of mentioning their wondrous story, that is, mention to those who ask you about the story of these young men, when they took refuge in the cave in the cave, and they descended in it, and took it as a shelter for them and a house to escape from their infidel people lest they be tempted in their religion, and they were seven young men with them. dog to them, so they said, asking their Lord: {Our Lord, give us mercy from Yourself and prepare for us guidance in our matter} meaning, give us mercy from You that will accompany us in this migration of ours from polytheism and the polytheists {and prepare for us guidance in our matter} i.e. Secret for us is our affair in our flight from the lands of the polytheists out of fear for our religion. of sound judgment} meaning righteousness, righteousness, and salvation from the people of disbelief and falsehood. Ibn Jarir al-Tabari said in his interpretation of these verses. The scholars differed as to the reason for the fate of these young men to the cave that God mentioned in His Book. Some of them said: The reason for that was that they were Muslims following the religion of Jesus and they had a king. An idol worshiper called them to worship idols, so they fled with their religion from him for fear that he would tempt them from their religion or kill them, so they hid from him in the cave, and God Almighty says: {So We struck their ears in the cave for a number of years} meaning, We struck their ears with a veil that prevented them from hearing sounds and movements, so they slept in their cave for a number of years. That is three hundred and nine For years, they were tossing and turning, with God's kindness and His provision for them, from side to side until He raised them from their sleep. This was God Almighty's response to them when they called upon Him, saying: "Our Lord, give us mercy from Yourself." And the Almighty says: "Then We raised them up," that is, from their sleep and slumber, "that We might know which of the two parties was more worthy." Why did they stay? That is, in the cave {for a period of time} meaning that we may know the knowledge of what is seen and that My servants may look and know which of the two groups that differed in the amount of their stay in the cave was calculated for the duration of their stay in the cave, as the people differed into two parties, one party saying they stayed in their cave for such and such a year and another saying they stayed for such and such an extent of time. The years.

Cave of the Seven Sleepers (Arabic: كهف الرقيم, Kahf ar-Raqim)

There is a historical and religious site in Al-Rajib, a village east of Amman. It is claimed that the cave housed the Seven Sleepers (Arabic: اشاب الكهف, aṣḥāb al kahf) – a group of youths who, according to Byzantine and Islamic sources, fled the religious persecution of the Roman emperor Decius. Legend has it that these people went into hiding in a cave around 250 AD, miraculously emerging some 200 or 300 years later. There remains considerable debate regarding the exact location of this cave – various locations in Turkey have been suggested, including Afsin, Tarsus and Mount Pion in addition to the al-Rajib site. The site is surrounded by the remains of two mosques and a large Byzantine cemetery. It is near Sabah Bus Station and about a fifteen minute bus journey from Amman's Vihdat Station.

When the youth retreated into the cave and said, 'Our Lord, grant us mercy from Yourself and prepare for us the right guidance from our matter.' So We put [a veil of sleep] on their ears inside the cave for many years. We then woke them up, so that we could show which of the two groups was the most accurate in calculating the extent to which they were still. It is We who tell you [O Muhammad], His story the truth. Verily, they were youths who believed in their Lord and We increased them in guidance.

Some argue that the place mentioned in Surah al-Kahf of the Qur'an is the cave of the seven sleepers.

The sura is named after the cave - al-Kahf - in honor of the supposed piety of the Seven Sleepers. The site's association with Islamic heritage led to the involvement of various Islamic leagues in its discovery and excavation. The cave was identified with the Qur'anic records because of the name of the nearby village of al-Rajib, which has a similar etymology to the word al-Raqim mentioned in al-Kahf. Some also argue the correspondence of the site with Surat al-Kahf based on the discovery of a dog skull near the entrance to the cave.

Origin of the name of the cave

The site's English name refers to the seven sleepers who sought refuge in the cave, although accounts differ widely regarding the number of sleepers. The canonical Islamic text refers to seven sleepers and one dog. The site's Arabic name, Arabic: كهف الرقيم, Kahf ar-Raqīm, is based on the triliteral root Arabic: ر-ق-م, denoting writing or calligraphy. It may refer to the village or the mountain in which the cave is located. It may also refer to the book in which the names of the seven sleepers are recorded, as suggested in Muhammad ibn Jarir al-Tabari's explanatory work Tafsir al-Tabari. The modern name of the nearby village, al-Rajib, may be a corruption of the word al-Raqim.

exploration and excavation

In 1951, the Jordanian journalist Taisir Thabyan discovered the Cave of the Seven Sleepers. He published the picture on the Journal of the Syrian Military Police before informing the Jordanian Antiquities Department. The department entrusted the work of research and exploration in the cave to Jordanian archaeologist Rafiq al-Dajani. They found eight smaller sealed tombs inside the main cave, in which the bones were preserved.

The cave of the seven sleepers is mentioned in a surah called Al-Kahf in the Holy Qur'an. The story concerns a group of youths escaping persecution by a local pagan ruler who fall asleep in a cave.

The Islamic version relates it to Surah (chapter) al-Kahf (18, "The Cave") of the Quran. During the time of Prophet Muhammad, the Jews of Medina challenged him to tell them the story of the sleepers, knowing that none of the Arabs knew about it. According to tradition, Allah sent the angel Gabriel (or Jibril) to reveal the story through Surah al-Kahf. After hearing this from him, the Jews confirmed that he told the same story that they knew.

Muhammad was challenged by the people of Mecca, who did not believe in his message and prophethood, with a question that the people of Mecca passed on to him from the Jews. The Jews knew that Muhammad would be able to tell the story only if he was indeed a prophet. The Jews asked the non-believers of Mecca to ask Muhammad "Who are the disappearing youths, and how many were they?". Mohammed had no clue and said he would answer them tomorrow, waiting for the answer to be revealed to him through Gabriel. However, the answer was revealed to Muhammad in a complete sura named the Cave of the Seven Sleepers (al-Kahf). The Qur'an revealed the exact story that the Jews knew, and it answered those questions (how young, and how many years disappeared) with the information they had. Quran confirms that they 309 slept for years, about which the Jews know. However, the Qur'an does not give an exact answer as to how many there were. It is mentioned that some people tell 3 or 5 or 7 apart from a dog. The Jews didn't know exactly how many those 3 or 5 or 7 were, and they were astounded when they learned that the Qur'an spelled out all those possible numbers for the sleepers.

The mention of the story in the Qur'an and the concurrent events that occurred before the story was revealed confirm the claim that the Qur'an was revealed by Allah and contains only the words of Allah and not the words of Muhammad, as it contains such information. Which Mohammed did not know.

The Qur'an states that the period of time these sleepers spent in the cave was three hundred years, during which the calendar of their people was changed from solar to lunar and

As a result, the duration of his sleep has increased to 309 (lunar). years. When they awoke, they did not know that they had slept for centuries and thought that they had only slept for a few hours. When he sent one of them to buy food, the coins he used to buy food went out of circulation and attracted the attention of the people of the city. After the story became widely known, the sleepers died. In the 18th chapter of the Qur'an, Surah Al Kahf, in the 18th verse, a dog is mentioned among those who sleep.

As long as they were asleep, you considered them to be awake, and We used to turn them to their right and left sides; surely turned back from them in flight, and would surely have been filled with terror from them.

(Surah Kahf, Quran: 18)

The ninth verse of Surah al-Kahf touches upon the exceptional position of this group. As the narrative unfolds, it is seen that his experiences are unusual and spiritual in nature. His whole life is full of miraculous developments. The tenth verse tells us that those youths took refuge in the cave from the existing oppressive system, which did not allow them to express their views, speak the truth and call on the religion of Allah. Thus, he distanced himself from his society.

كهف أهل الكهف
(قبور بيزنطية) وردت تصنيم في القرآن الكريم
CAVE OF THE SEVEN SLEEPERS
BYZANTINE TOMBS.. ONE MENTIONED
IN THE KORAN IN THE STORY OF THE
SEVEN SLEEPERS

Do you believe that the Companions of the Cave and Ar-Raqim were the most notable of Our signs? When the youths took refuge in the cave and said: 'Our Lord, direct us Your mercy and open for us the right guidance in our situation. (Surah Al Kahf, Quran: 9-10)

 So we closed their ears with sleep for many years in the cave. Then we woke them up again, so we could see which of the two gangs could better calculate the time they stayed there. (Surah Al Kahf, Quran: 11-12)

The reason for this state of sleep was his submission to fate and peace, because Allah arranges everything for the benefit of the believers.

 The Qur'an also says that the number of sleepers will be known to Allah, and only a handful of people. It is not mentioned that there were seven sleepers.

 They will say: "There were three of them, their dog was the fourth." And they would say, "There were seven of them, the eighth being their dog." Say, "My Lord knows best their numbers." There are very few who know about him.' So do not enter into any dispute about him except that which is clearly known. And don't take any of them's opinion about them. (Surat Al Kahf, Quran: 22)"

Reference - Spain

7 Holy Youths The "Seven Sleepers" of Ephesus

Troparion and Kontakion

The seven youths of Ephesus: Maximilian, Iamblichus, Martinian, John, Dionysius, Exacustodianus (Constantine) and Antoninus, lived in the 3rd century. Saint Maximilian was the son of the administrator of the city of Ephesus, and the other six youths were the sons of eminent citizens of Ephesus. These youths were friends from childhood, and all were in military service together.

When Emperor Decius (249-251) arrived in Ephesus, he ordered all citizens to offer sacrifices to the pagan gods. Anyone who did not obey was subjected to torture and death. The informers slandered the seven youths and summoned them to answer the charges. Appearing before the emperor, the youths confessed their faith in Christ.Their military belts and insignia were immediately taken away from them. Decius allowed them to go free, however, he hoped that they would change their minds when he went on a military campaign. The youths fled the city and hid in a cave on Mount Ochlon, where they spent their time in prayer, preparing for martyrdom.

The youngest of them, Saint Iamblichus, disguised himself as a beggar and went into the city to buy bread. During his excursion into the city, he heard that the emperor had returned and was looking for them. Saint Maximilian urged his companions to come out of the cave and present themselves for trial.

Upon discovering where the youths were hiding, the emperor ordered that the entrance to the cave be blocked with stones so that the saints would die of hunger and thirst. The two dignitaries present at the entrance to the cave were secret Christians. Wishing to preserve the memory of the saints, they placed a sealed container in the cave containing two metal plaques. They bore the names of seven young men and details of their suffering and death.The Lord put the youths into a miraculous sleep that lasted for nearly two centuries. In the meantime, the persecution against Christians had ceased. During the reign of the holy emperor Theodosius the Younger (408-450) there were heretics who denied that there would be a general resurrection of the dead at the second coming of our Lord Jesus Christ. Some of them said, "How can there be a resurrection of the dead when there will be neither soul nor body, since they have disintegrated?" Others affirmed, "Only souls will receive restoration, for it will be impossible for bodies to rise and live after a thousand years, when not even their dust will remain."

Therefore, the Lord revealed the secret of the resurrection and future life of the dead through seven of His saints.

The owner of the land on which Mount Ochlon was situated discovered the stone formation, and his workers opened the entrance to the cave. God had kept the youths alive, and they awoke from their sleep, unaware that nearly two hundred years had passed. Their bodies and clothes were completely untouched.Preparing to accept torture, the young men once again asked Saint Iamblikus to buy bread for them in the city. Approaching the city, the young man was surprised to see a cross on the gate. Hearing the name of Jesus Christ spoken openly, he began to suspect that he was approaching his own city.

When he paid for the bread, Iamblikus gave the merchant coins bearing the image of the emperor Decius. He was detained, as he could hide a pile of old money. They took Saint Iamblikus to the city administrator, who was also the bishop of Ephesus. Hearing the young man's puzzling answers, the bishop felt that God was revealing some kind of secret through him, and he went with the others to the cave.

At the entrance to the cave the bishop found a sealed container and opened it. He read on the metal plaques the names of the seven young men and a description of the sealing of the cave on the orders of the emperor Decius. Going into the cave and seeing the saints alive, everyone rejoiced and realized that the Lord, by awakening them from their long sleep, was showing the Church the mystery of the resurrection of the dead.Soon the emperor himself arrived in Ephesus and spoke to the youths in the cave. Then the holy youths, in full view of everyone, lowered their heads to the ground and fell asleep again, this time until the general resurrection.

The emperor wanted to put each of the youths in a jeweled coffin, but they appeared to him in a dream and said that their bodies should be left on the ground in the cave. In the XII century the Russian pilgrim Igumen Daniel saw the holy relics of the seven youths in the cave.

The second memory of the seven youths is celebrated on October 22. According to a tradition, which is recorded in the Russian Prologue (Lives of the Saints), on this day the youths fell asleep for the second time. The Greek Menaion of 1870 states that they fell asleep for the first time on August 4, and woke up on October 22.The Great Book of Needs (Trebnik) contains a prayer to the Seven Sleepers of Ephesus for those who are sick and cannot sleep. The Seven Sleepers are also mentioned in the church New Year service, September 1.

Memory of the Holy Youths of Ephesus "The Seven Sleepers"

The Orthodox Church

Today, August 4, commemorates St. John the Younger, the Martyr Ia and the 9,000 people who died with her in Persia, as well as the holy seven youths in Ephesus (Maximilian, Iamblichus, Martinian, John, Dionysius, Exacustodianus and Antoninus), who awoke from a long sleep.

In the middle of the third century A.D., the emperor Decius tortured and killed young and old Christians indiscriminately. At that time, the seven youths did not want to deny their faith in the Trinity, so after first giving their property to the poor, they left the city and hid in a cave until the persecution stopped.

But as the danger was approaching, they prayed to the Holy Spirit, and if God allows it, they asked to take their souls so that they would not fall alive into the hands of Decius. God heard their prayers and recognized their pure intentions. Therefore, after going to bed at night, they did not wake up in the morning.194 years later, under Theodosius the Younger, a sect in Ephesus declared that there would be no resurrection of the dead. At that time, the youngest of the 7 youths of Ephesus bought bread with a coin used in the time of Decius. They arrested him immediately. This was not surprising.

After interrogating him, they went to the cave and found the other six youths alive.

Then, everyone understood that this was a miracle and a true intervention of God, and so, even those who were skeptical at first eventually came to believe that the resurrection of the dead and the Second Coming were real facts. Christians believe in and accept the Creed, which affirms the resurrection of the dead.

Source: Cyprus Church

Historical and religious background

Historical and religious background of the legend in the 5th century

The plot of the legend begins in the middle of the 3rd century, during the reign of the Roman emperor Decius. 6 He was described as a good emperor, and senatorial historians regarded him as the embodiment of the old Roman virtues. In January 250, Decius issued an edict for the suppression of Christianity, requiring all citizens of the Roman Empire to make sacrifices, offerings to the gods, the completion of which was the basis for issuing a certificate - libellus. However, the purpose of this edict was not to exterminate Christians, but to make them loyal citizens participating in all forms of state worship. It had a mainly propaganda and anti-democratic character and claimed to show the ideological unity of the empire in the face of invaders, especially the Goths, who defeated and killed Decius during the Battle of Abritus. This order was prepared for a relatively long time and was gradually implemented in different areas.7 The time of the awakening of the sleepers fell on the politically and religiously turbulent time of the reign of Theodosius II, usually called the Younger. Unlike his grandfather Theodosius the Great, who fought mainly with Arianism, Theodosius the Younger exterminated paganism and destroyed many temples and monuments of pagan culture. During his reign there were major disputes within Christianity regarding the understanding of the nature of Christ. They saw in Christ two substances (ousias from the Greek ousia), two hypostases (qneume, in Greek hypostasis) and one person (parsufo, in Greek prosopon). Nestoriusdid not mention Kyno (in Greek Phsis), so he was considered to have understood the Cunum as persons at the Ephesian Council. This conflict at the level of Christology, one of the longest-lasting conflicts in Christianity, was finally resolved in 1994 by the proclamation of the Common Christological Declaration between the Catholic Church and the Assyrian Church of the East. Both churches also recognized the validity and accuracy of the manifestations of the Christotokos and the Theotokos. 6 Imperator Caesar Gaius Messius Quintus Traianus Decius Augustus, 249-251 A.D. 7 M. Jaczynowska, Dzieje Imperium Romanum, Warszawa 1995, p. 35148 Bartłomiej Grysa

It is worth noting that the Assyrian Church of the East never considered itself "Nestorian". Eutyches (370-455), the head of a large monastery in Constantinople, was the second person who caused a serious theological controversy within the Church. In the fight against Nestorius he was one of the most ardent supporters of Cyril of Alexandria, who was entrusted by Pope St. Celestine i with the task of executing a sentence passed on Nestorius.8 He enjoyed considerable influence at the imperial court thanks to his godson, Crizaph, an influential minister of the emperor. After Eutyches was denounced before Patriarch Flavian he was asked to explain his Christological views. Persecuted by the members of the patriarchal synod he appealed to the pope and the patriarchs of Alexandria and Jerusalem for their assistance. Theodosius II also interceded for him before the pope, who called him a very inexperienced and foolish old man. While the views of Eutyches were indeed Monophysite, the Christology of the Churches of Egypt, Syria and Armenia, which were attributed these views, would be called Miaphysite after Cyril's famous formula: mia physis tou Theo Logou Sacerkomene - the one nature of the incarnate Word of God. Here again we come to the aid only after many centuries when the Common Declaration of Pope John Paul II and His Holiness Mar Ignatius Zakka I Iwas proclaimed in 1984, confirming the theological correctness of the above-mentioned formula and seeing the reasons for the division actually in "differences in terminology and culture and in different formulas adopted by different theological schools to express the same matter."9 Comparison of some texts of the legend The Syrian texts are perhaps the oldest original material for the legend of the Seven Sleepers, written at the beginning of the 6th century, that is, about one hundred years before the rise of Islam. A common version of the various Christian and Muslim accounts could be as follows: for some reason several young men took refuge in a cave, where they fell asleep. After several years they were raised to become a divine sign of hope for resurrection.It seemed to these young men that they were at their hideout for a very short time, for one day, but in reality they had been sleeping there for several years. After awakening the brothers sent one of their companions to the city where he could buy food. There are, however, significant differences in the texts of the two traditions. They are linked by the theological nature of the legend, and even though they 291. 9 "Common Declaration of Pope John Paul II and His Holiness Mar Ignatius Zakka I Iwas (October 27, 1971)," Acta Apostolicae Sedis 63 (1971), pp. 814-815.are not related to the truth of the resurrection in general, which both Christians and Muslims admit, they are mainly related to the religion of those brothers. The Syriac texts followed by all Christians state that these brothers were persecuted by Decius for their faith in Christ. The persecution in the days of Decius is confirmed by all historical sources. On the other hand, the Quran, which is followed by some other Arabic sources, does not specify the religion of those brothers, describing them generally as "believers" or "believers in God." At-Tabari writes that the brothers came from "people who worshiped the Roman gods." However, Allah led them to the true faith - Islam. Their law10 was the law of 'Isa11 A similar "objection" also occurs when Malchus - the minister of the brothers - goes to the city for food. One of the official Arabic texts extant in Egypt states that he saw on every gate of the city a sign "which belongs only to those who believe."12 Syrian sources explicitly specify that this sign was the cross. There is no consensus in the texts about the number of the brothers or their names: sometimes they were three, sometimes five, seven or even eight.13 They probably belong to somewhat different traditions: Jews and western Assyrians ("Jacobites") from Nagaran believed that they were three. Yet eastern Assyrians ("Nestorians") argued that there were five.14 At-Tabari gives the number of brothers as seven, eight or nine, along with a dog,15 which is supported by orthodox Muslim tradition, according to which the eighth brother was a dog named ar-Raqim16 or Qitmir. Such a hypothesis is a serious concern becauseAt-Tabari states that ar-Rākīm is the name of a tablet on which an inscription was engraved. The tablet was placed at the entrance of the cave or kept in a box in the middle of it by the brothers.17 It is doubtful whether the term was used in the third century. 10 In Arabic: šarī'a, meaning law in general or Koranic law in particular. 11 M. at-Tabari, Taṣrī' ar-rusūl wal-mulūk, Beirut 1989, p. 455, part 1. Furthermore, the phrase "the law of Christ" has no basis in the Gospels or in church history. Jesus himself said that he came not to abolish the Law (the Law of Moses) but to fulfill it (see Matthew 5:17). 12 M. Baranīk, Ahl al-Kahf, [in:] Maghmu'at al-qishas ad-diniya, Cairo 1987, p. 21. The adopted names of the 13 brothers are in various versions as follows: Maximilian, Malchus, Martinian, Dionysius, John, Serapion, Constantine, Anthony; Malchus, Maximian, Martinian, Dionysius, John, Serapion, Constantine; Yamblikh, Maximilian, Martinian, Dionysius, John, Constantine, Anthony;

Achilleides, Diomedes, Diogenes, Probatus, Stephanus, Sambatus, Quiriacus (according to St. Gregory of Tours); Yamalia (Yamani), Makimilina (Maximilina, Machimilina), Mislina, Marnush (Marus), Sannus, Dabranus (Bironos), Kaphastius (Kossonos), Samonos, Butonos, Kalos, Qumeir (the name of a dog; according to at-Sabri and ad-Damiri);   Ikileos, Dionysios, Istifanos, Fructis, Sebastos, Qiriakos (according to the history of Michael the Syrian); Arcelitis, Diometeos, Sabastios, Probatios, Avainios, Stephanos, Kyriakos (in Coptic according to I. Guidi, op. cit., p. 14). 14 M. Gaudefroy-Demombynes, Narodzini Islamu, op. cit., p. 319. 15 M. Aḥt-Sabari, Tārih ar-Rusūl wal-Muluk, op. cit., part 1, p. 454. 16 M. Gaudefroy-Demombynes, Narodzini Islamu, op. cit., p. 319. 17 M. Aḥt-Sabari, Tārih ar-Rusūl wal-Muluk, op. cit., part 1, p. 45

Number and names

Jewish and Christian versions

Early versions do not all agree on or even specify the number of sleepers. Some Jewish circles and the Christians of Najran believed in only three brothers; the East Syriac, five. Most Syriac accounts have eight, including a nameless watcher which God sets over the sleepers. A 6th-century Latin text titled "Pilgrimage of Theodosius"featured the sleepers as seven people in number, with a dog named Viricanus.

Bartłomiej Grysa lists at least seven different sets of names for the sleepers:

Maximian, Martinian, Dionisius, John, Constantine, Malchus, Serapion

Maximilian, Martinian, Dionisius, John, Constantine, Malkhus, Serapion, Anthony

Maximilian, Martinian, Dionisius, John, Constantine, Yamblikh (Iamblichus), Anthony

Makṯimilīnā (Maksimilīnā, Maḥsimilīnā), Marnūš (Marṭūs), Kafaštaṭyūš (Ksōṭōnos), Yamlīḫā (Yamnīḫ), Mišlīnā, Saḏnūš,

Dabranūš (Bīrōnos), Samōnos, Buṭōnos, Qālos (according to aṭ-Ṭabarī and ad-Damīrī)

Achillides, Probatus, Stephanus, Sambatus, Quiriacus, Diogenus, Diomedes (according to Gregory of Tours)

Ikilios, Fruqtis, Istifanos, Sebastos, Qiryaqos, Dionisios (according to Michael the Syrian)

Aršellītīs, Probatios, Sabbastios, Stafanos, Kīriakos, Diōmetios, Avhenios (according to the Coptic version)

Islamic view

In Islam no specific number is mentioned. Qur'an 18:22 discusses the disputes regarding their numbers. The verse says:

Some will say, "They were three, their dog was the fourth," while others will say, "They were five, their dog was the sixth," only guessing blindly. And others will say, "They were seven and their dog was the eighth." Say, O Prophet, "My Lord knows best their exact number. Only a few people know as well." So do not argue about them except with sure knowledge, nor consult any of those who debate about them.[failed verification][dubious – discuss]

Caves of the Seven Sleepers

Several sites are attributed as the "Cave of the Seven Sleepers", but none could empirically convince to be the original site associated with the legend. As the earliest versions of the legend spread out from Ephesus, an early Christian catacomb in that area came to be associated with it, attracting scores of pilgrims. On the slopes of Mount Pion (Mount Coelian) near Ephesus (near modern Selçuk in Turkey), the grotto of the Seven Sleepers with ruins of the religious site built over it was excavated in 1926–1928.:394 The excavation brought to light several hundred graves dated to the 5th and 6th centuries. Inscriptions dedicated to the Seven Sleepers were found on the walls and in the graves. This grotto is still shown to tourists.

Other possible sites of the cave of the Seven Sleepers are in Damascus, Syria and Afşin and Tarsus, Turkey. Afşin is near the antique Roman city of Arabissus, to which the East Roman Emperor Justinian paid a visit. The site was a Hittite temple, used as a Roman temple and later as a church in Roman and Byzantine times. The Emperor brought marble niches from Western Anatolia as gifts for it, which are preserved inside the Eshab-ı Kehf Kulliye mosque to this day. The Seljuks continued to use the place of worship as a church and a mosque. It was turned into a mosque over time, with the conversion of the local population to Islam.

There is a cave near Amman, Jordan, also known as the Cave of Seven Sleepers, which has eight smaller sealed tombs present inside and a ventilation duct coming out of the cave.

List of notable sites

Asia Minor

Eshab-ı Kehf Cave , Ephesus, Turkey
Eshab-ı Kehf Cave, Tarsus, Turkey
Grotto of the Seven Sleepers, İzmir, Turkey
Eshab-ı Kehf Kulliye, outside Afşin, Turkey
MENA region

Mar Musa, monastery in Syria
Mount Qasioun, Damascus, Syria
Cave of the Seven Sleepers, Al-Rajeb (Greater Amman), Jordan
Mosquée de Sept Dormants, Chenini, Tunisia
China

Tuyuq Khojam Mazar, Turpan, China

Entrance to the cave, near Amman, Jordan

Eshab-ı Kehf Kulliye in Afşin with the cave inside, Turkey

Eshab-ı Kehf Cave in Tarsus, Turkey

Description

The site consists at its core of a rock-hewn ancient burial cave with multiple burials. Some 500 metres west of the cave is a Byzantine cemetery.

The cave is partly natural, partly man-made. The entrance to the cave is flanked by two stone pilasters and two niches, one on each side, vestiges of a Byzantine church. The entrance is from the south, and above it are the remains of a mirab (niche), once part of a mosque. Next to it are traces of a minaret, as well as four Byzantine pillars. An Arabic inscription states that this mosque, the second at the site, was built by orders of the son of Ahmad ibn Tulun, the founder of the Tulunid dynasty (r. 868–884). Archaeologists have concluded that here a Byzantine church was converted into a mosque in the time of Umayyad caliph Abd al-Malik ibn Marwan (d. 705), which underwent renovation under the Tulunids.

The cave contains seven sarcophagi. A hole has been carved through one of them, allowing a look at the bones buried inside. A wall inscription contains the basmala as well as verses from the Qur'an carved in Kufic script. Christian and Islamic symbols are also visible on the walls.

The Seven Sleepers

Bible Stories and Religious Classics — Philip P. Wells

The seven sleepers were born in the city of Ephesus. And when Decius the emperor came into Ephesus for the persecution of Christian men, he commanded to edify the temples in the middle of the city, so that all should come with him to do sacrifice to the idols, and did do seek all the Christian people, and bind them for to make them to do sacrifice, or else to put them to death; in such wise that every man was afeard of the pains that he promised, that the friend forsook his friend, and the son renied his father, and the father the son. And then in this city were founden seven Christian men, that is to wit, Maximian, Malchus, Marcianus, Denis, John, Serapion, and Constantine. And when they saw this, they had much sorrow, and because they were the first in the palace that despised the sacrifices, they hid them in their houses, and were in fastings and in prayers. And then they were accused tofore Decius, and came thither, and were found very Christian men. Then was given to them space for to repent them, unto the coming again of Decius. And in the meanwhile they dispended their patrimony in alms to the poor people; and assembled them together, and took counsel, and went to the mount of Celion, and there ordained to be more secretly, and there hid them long time. And one of them administered and served them always. And when he went into the city, he clothed him in the habit of a beggar.

When Decius was come again, he commanded that they should be fetched, and then Malchus, which was their servant and ministered to them meat and drink, returned in great dread to his fellows, and told and showed to them the great fury and woodness of them, and then were they sore afraid. And Malchus set tofore them the loaves of bread that he had brought, so that they were comforted of the meat, and were more strong for to suffer torments. And when they had taken their refection and sat in weeping and wailings, suddenly, as God would, they slept, and when it came on the morn they were sought and could not be found. Wherefore Decius was sorrowful because he had lost such young men. And then they were accused that they were hid in the mount of Celion, and had given their goods to poor men, and yet abode in their purpose. And then commanded Decius that their kindred should come to him, and menaced them to the death if they said not of them all that they knew. And they accused them, and complained that they had dispended all their riches. Then Decius thought what he should do with them, and, as our Lord would, he inclosed the mouth of the cave wherein they were with stones, to the end that they should die therein for hunger and fault of meat. Then the ministers and two Christian men, Theodorus and Rufinus, wrote their martyrdom and laid it subtlely among the stones. And when Decius was dead, and all that generation, three hundred and sixty-two years after, and the thirtieth year of Theodosius the emperor, when the heresy was of them that denied the resurrection of dead bodies, and began to grow; Theodosius, then the most Christian emperor, being sorrowful that the faith of our Lord was so felonously demened, for anger and heaviness he clad him in hair and wept every day in a secret place, and led a full holy life, which God, merciful and piteous, seeing, would comfort them that were sorrowful and weeping, and give to them esperance and hope of the resurrection of dead men, and opened the precious treasure of his pity, and raised the foresaid martyrs in this manner following.

He put in the will of a burgess of Ephesus that he would make in that mountain, which was desert and aspre, a stable for his pasturers and herdmen. And it happed that of adventure the masons, that made the said stable, opened this cave. And then these holy saints, that were within, awoke and were raised and intersalued each other, and had supposed verily that they had slept but one night only, and remembered of the heaviness that they had the day tofore. And then Malchus, which ministered to them, said what Decius had ordained of them, for he said: We have been sought, like as I said to you yesterday, for to do sacrifice to the idols, that is it that the emperor desireth of us. And then Maximian answered: God our Lord knoweth that we shall never sacrifice, and comforted his fellows. He commanded to Malchus to go and buy bread in the city, and bade him bring more that he did yesterday, and also to inquire and demand what the emperor had commanded to do. And then Malchus took five shillings, and issued out of the cave, and when he saw the masons and the stones tofore the cave, he began to bless him, and was much amarvelled. But he thought little on the stones, for he thought on other things. Then came he all doubtful to the gates of the city, and was all amarvelled. For he saw the sign of the cross about the gate, and then, without tarrying, he went to that other gate of the city, and found there also the sign of the cross thereon, and then he had great marvel, for upon every gate he saw set up the sign of the cross; and therewith the city was garnished. And then he blessed him and returned to the first gate, and weened he had dreamed; and after he advised and comforted himself and covered his visage and entered into the city. And when he came to the sellers of bread, and heard the men speak of God, yet then was he more abashed, and said: What is this, that no man yesterday durst name Jesu Christ, and now every man confesseth him to be Christian? I trow this is not the city of Ephesus, for it is all otherwise builded. It is some other city, I wot not what.

And when he demanded and heard verily that it was Ephesus, he supposed that he had erred, and thought verily to go again to his fellows, and then went to them that sold bread. And when he showed his money the sellers marvelled, and said that one to that other, that this young man had found some old treasure. And when

Malchus saw them talk together, he doubted not that they would lead him to the emperor, and was sore afeard, and prayed them to let him go, and keep both money and bread, but they held him, and said to him: Of whence art thou? For thou hast found treasure of old emperors, show it to us, and we shall be fellows with thee and keep it secret. And Malchus was so afeard that he wist not what to say to them for dread. And when they saw that he spake not they put a cord about his neck, and drew him through the city unto the middle thereof. And tidings were had all about in the city that a young man had found ancient treasure, in such wise that all they of the city assembled about him, and he confessed there that he had found no treasure. And he beheld them all, but he could know no man there of his kindred ne lineage, which he had verily supposed that they had lived, but found none, wherefore he stood as he had been from himself, in the middle of the city. And when St. Martin the bishop, and Antipater the consul, which were new come into this city, heard of this thing they sent for him, that thcy should bring him wisely to them, and his money with him. And when he was brought to the church he weened well he should have been led to the Emperor Decius. And then the bishop and the consul marvelled of the money, and they demanded him where he had found this treasure unknown. And he answered that he had nothing founden, but it was come to him of his kindred and patrimony, and they demanded of him of what city he was. I wot well that I am of this city, if this be the city of Ephesus. And the judge said to him: Let thy kindred come and witness for thee. And he named them, but none knew them. And they said that he feigned, for to escape from them in some manner. And then said the judge: How may we believe thee that this money is come to thee of thy friends, when it appeareth in the scripture that it is more than three hundred and seventy-two years sith it was made and forged, and is of the first days of Decius the emperor, and it resembleth nothing to our money; and how may it come from thy lineage so long since, and thou art young, and wouldst deceive the wise and ancient men of this city of Ephesus? And therefore I command that thou be demened after the law till thou hast confessed where thou hast found this money. Then Malchus kneeled down tofore them and said: For God's sake, lords, say ye to me that I shall demand you, and I shall tell to you all that I have in my heart. Decius the emperor that was in this city, where is he? And the bishop said to him there is no such at this day in the world that is named Decius, he was emperor many years since. And Malchus said: Sire, hereof I am greatly abashed and no man believeth me, for I wot well that we fled for fear of Decius the emperor, and I saw him, that yesterday he entered into this city, if this be the city of Ephesus. Then the bishop thought in himself, and said to the judge that, this is a vision that our Lord will have showed by this young man. Then said the young man: Follow ye me, and I shall show to you my fellows which be in the mount of Celion, and believe ye them. This know I well, that we fled from the face of the Emperor Decius. And then they went with him, and a great multitude of the people of the city with them. And Malchus entered first into the cave to his fellows, and the bishop next after him. And there found they among the stones the letters sealed with two seals of silver. And then the bishop called them that were come thither, and read them tofore them all, so that they that heard it were all abashed and amarvelled. And they saw the saints sitting in the cave, and their visages like unto roses flowering, and they, kneeling down, glorified God. And anon the bishop and the judge sent to Theodosius the emperor, praying him that he would come anon for to see the marvels of our Lord that he had late showed. And anon he arose up from the ground, and took off the sack in which he wept, and glorified our Lord. And came from Constantinople to Ephesus, and all they came against him, and ascended in to the mountain with him together, unto the saints in to the cave.

And as soon as the blessed saints of our Lord saw the emperor come, their visages shone like to the sun. And the emperor entered then, and glorified our Lord and embraced them, weeping upon each of them, and said: I see you now like as I should see our Lord raising Lazarus. And then Maximian said to him: Believe us, for forsooth our Lord hath raised us tofore the day of the great resurrection. And to the end that thou believe firmly the resurrection of the dead people, verily we be raised as ye here see, and live. And in like wise as the child is in the womb of his mother without feeling harm or hurt, in the same wise we have been living and sleeping in lying here without feeling of anything. And when they had said all this, they inclined their heads to the earth, and rendered their spirits at the command of our Lord Jesu Christ, and so died. Then the emperor arose, and fell on them, weeping strongly, and embraced them, and kissed them debonairly. And then he commanded to make precious sepulchres of gold and silver, and to bury their bodies therein. And in the same night they appeared to the emperor, and said to him that he should suffer them to lie on the earth like as they had lain tofore till that time that our Lord had raised them, unto the time that they should rise again. Then commanded the emperor that the place should be adorned nobly and richly with precious stones, and all the bishops that would confess the resurrection should be assoiled. It is in doubt of that which is said that they slept three hundred and sixty-two years, for they were raised the year of our Lord four hundred and seventy-eight, and Decius reigned but one year and three months, and that was in the year of our Lord two hundred and seventy, and so they slept but two hundred and eight years.

GROTTO OF THE SEVEN SLEEPERS IN EPHESUS: MYTH OR REAL

Caves and mountains have always fascinated the human mind. There seems to be something about the earth opening up or rising to tower above all else that triggers our spiritual predisposition. As a result, many caves and mountains across the globe are considered sacred by their respective communities, whether as the homes of gods and spirits or as portals to other mysterious worlds.

In a country with such a rich religious history as Turkey, one such cave sits on Mount Pion near the ruins of Ephesus. For centuries, the cave has fascinated and attracted pilgrims from all over the world and has been the source of several religious myths. Today, it is better known as Grotto of the Seven Sleepers (Yedi Uyuyanlar Magarasi), after the most famous legend, the Christian version.

The Legend

Generally, the legend tells the story of a group of youths who hid/slept in a cave and woke up years later to find that the world had changed. The most popular iteration is the Christian legend of Grotto of the Seven Sleepers begins at around 250 CE and extends to approximately 408 CE.

Seven Sleepers in Christianity
Christian Version

This legend is set when Christianity was on the rise, facing widespread persecution in the Roman Era. Trajan Decius (249 to 251 CE), the Roman Emperor, was a pagan true to his Roman gods. Thus, he came to the city of Ephesus to enforce his laws against Christianity.

At around this time, seven young Christian men were allowed to renounce their faith and bow to the Roman gods. Depending on the source, these young men are believed to be Martin, Maximilian, John, Jamplichos, Exakostodianos, Dionysios, and Antoninos.

Emperor Decius gave them some time for consideration until his return to Ephesus. But ever adamant, the young men refused to renounce Christianity. Instead, they distributed their possessions among the poor of Ephesus and went to hide and pray in a mountain cave, during which they were overcome by significant sleepiness.

The young men were later discovered sleeping in the cave, and at the behest of Decius, the cave's entrance was sealed. Another version of the story tells that the emperor had the group locked up in the shelter as punishment for their Christian belief. All in all, a group of Christians is sleeping in a cave with a sealed entrance.

Many years passed, and the local population forgot about the incident. Then, some 158-200 years later, during the reign of Emperor Theodosius II (r408 CE to 450 CE), a landowner wanted to use the cave as a cowshed. Thus, he demolished the walled-up entrance and was surprised to find seven sleeping men inside.

Another version tells that the entrance collapsed after an earthquake hit the area.

Even more surprising is what the freshly woken men believed; they thought that they had slept for just a day. However, they were pretty hungry and thus, sent one of them to Ephesus to buy some food. During his errand, he had to be extremely careful to avoid getting caught by the Pagans.

As he made his way through the metropolis, the young man was astonished to see crosses on buildings. The Ephesians were even more surprised when he tried to pay for food using ancient coins from the reign of Decius. It turns out it was 158-200 years after they fell asleep in the cave, and Christianity was now the official religion of the Roman Empire.

After hearing their story, the inhabitants of Ephesus called the local bishop who met the seven sleepers, who later died from natural causes. Their miraculous experience moved the emperor Theodosius II, who ordered that their bodies be richly enshrined. Thus, the legend of the seven sleepers quickly propagated throughout the Christian world, making the cave a place of pilgrimage for the next 1000 years.

Seven Sleepers in Islam

The Islamic version

Unsurprisingly, an Islamic version of the legend of the seven sleepers also developed some time later. This version is even quoted in the Koran in Sura 18, verses 9 to 26, making it quite popular in the Muslim world. However, the Koran doesn't specify the cave's location nor the number of men found sleeping.

According to this iteration, the young men (referred to as 'the people of the cave') slept for 300 or 309 years. A dog also accompanied the men on their journey to the cave and then slept at the entrance. All who passed near the cave saw the dog but were afraid to look inside as they thought it was guarding the cave's secrets.

Overall, it's pretty similar to the Christian legend in that.

The protagonists of the story were sons of wealthy and noblemen. They lived in a kingdom a wash with idle worship and where belief in a single supreme deity was discouraged and punishable.

The region's ruler gave them some time to renounce their faith, which they refused to do. Thus, they retreated to a cave to hide.

Once in the cave, the youth were overcome by sleep and slumbered for centuries.

Is the legend of the Seven Sleepers true?

While there isn't a shortage of people who believe in the legend of the Seven Sleepers, we can't tell for sure whether it's true or not. This is because it hasn't been archeologically proven that the cave (grotto) on the slopes of Mount Pion is the cave of sleepers.

What archeologists have found is a valuable collection of terracotta lamps decorated with incredible scenes from the old testament, everyday Roman life, and Greek mythology. They've also discovered hundreds of graves from the 5th and 6th centuries CE, indicating that this area must've been an extensive Byzantine necropolis.

Varying beliefs

The earliest version of the story (by the Syrian bishop Jacob of Serug) is believed to have been derived from a now-lost Greek source. Most people associate the legend with the cave at Mt.Pion because the earliest versions of the tale spread from the ancient city of Ephesus. However, there remains a possibility that the earliest versions referred to a different cave.

Other sites for this (supposedly) miraculous event include Afsin and Tarsus in present-day Turkey, a cave near Amman in Jordan, and even China. So, there is no clear consensus on whether the events happened and where they happened.

On the other hand, some people believe there may be some truth behind this story since similar versions of the seven sleepers appear in British, Indian, Jewish, German, and Slavic traditions. Moreover, the fact that the story is a worldwide phenomenon may well be a strong case for the story's accuracy.

But all in all, we know that for around a thousand years, the legend of the seven sleepers was considered genuine by Christians from the Roman and Byzantine empires. They also believed that the cave at Mount Pion was where the young men lay undisturbed for up to 150 years. Thus, it became the Grotto of the Seven Sleepers, a sacred destination for pilgrims from all over Christendom.

Qitmir (dog)

In Islamic tradition, Qitmir was the dog that guarded the People of the Cave and stood by them all through their long sleep. His name, Qitmir, in Arabic is the name of a small membrane on separating a date from its seed. He is sometimes called Ar-Raqim , although narrations identify that Ar-Raqim was the name of the cave, or the name of a "brass plate, or stone table".

He is regarded as one of the most important animals of Islam. In Tafsir Ibn Kathir, Ibn Jurayj described Qitmir as lying outside the door on his stomach with his front legs stretched out. He was also said to be either the hunting dog of one of the Companions of the Cave, which is the more accepted view, or the dog of the king's chef, who accepted the Ashābul-Kahf's religious views, and brought Qitmir with him.

In the Quran

In Al-Kahf, the following is mentioned:

And you would have thought they were awake, while they were actually asleep. And We turned them on their right and on their left sides, and their dog stretching forth his two forelegs at the entrance [of the Cave]. Had you looked at them, you would certainly have run away from them, and would certainly have been filled with awe of them.

Alleged skull

Arab archaeologist Rafiq Al-Dajani entered the Cave of the Seven Sleepers in Al-Rajib in 1963, where he allegedly found seven graves, and part of a dog's skull on the door of the cave.

My another books

Sr N.	Book
1	World's Major religions, doctrines and sects
2	An introduction to the Holy Qur'an and it's unsolved mysteries
3	How did humans and language originate ?
4	Islam an introduction and sect
5	Sermons of great people
6	Prayer
7	Allah an introduction
8	Is Al khizr still alive today?
9	Story of harut and marut
10	Grief
11	The mysterious story of Al kahf (Ar raqim)
12	Naming of God
13	Who was Sheeba?
14	Death concept of the Holy Quran

30	For Divorce! Who is responsible?
31	Hadith to denomination
32	Karma is the best?
33	According to dreams, religion and science
34	End day

All these books are available in Hindi language and other international languages and are also available in e-book for **free on Google Play** Store.
All the books are available in paper back edition and hard cover edition as well.
These books are also available on Amazon, Flipkart and notionpress.com.

My personal introduction

My name is Abdul Waheed, my father's name is Late Haji Ubaidur Rahman and mother's name is Jaibunnisa. I have liked scientific ideology since childhood and have a calm nature and attachment to books. Due to which my curiosity interest has been continuously used in new discoveries and information. I got selected in polytechnic while doing BSc, but unfortunately it remained incomplete because father and brother died. Two words of my father, which are very precious for my life,

<u>first - earn honestly, do not take support of lies,</u>

<u>secondly, respect food and eat as much as you want.</u> That's why the education remained incomplete due to the responsibility of the house, then later getting married. Still did not lose courage and today the book is available in front of you in the form of my thoughts. If any information is left incomplete, please let us know.

Thank you .

Contact-

AbdulWaheed,Barabanki,Uttarpradesh, India

://www.facebook.com/profile.php?id=100091298026218